Boggart San

Best wishes
Martin Riley

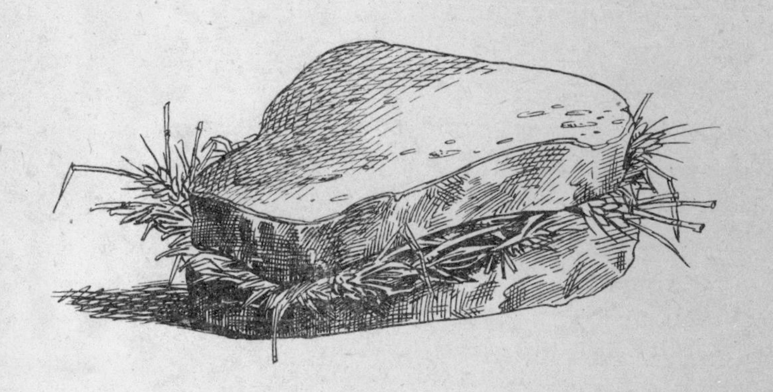

Boggart Sandwich

Martin Riley

Boggarty Boggarty Boo!
We want to be friends with you!
Wild and Witchery,
Tricksy, Twitchery,
Hairy, Tattery,
Mad as a Hattery,
Boggarty Boggarty Boo!

Illustrated by Chris Riddell

BBC Books

Map devised by Julie Robinson

Published by BBC Books,
a division of BBC Enterprises Limited,
Woodlands, 80 Wood Lane, London W12 0TT

First published 1989

ISBN 0 563 20871 6

Set in 13/14pt Bembo by Ace Filmsetting Ltd, Frome, Somerset
Printed and bound in Great Britain by Richard Clay Ltd, Bungay
Cover printed by Richard Clay Ltd, Norwich

Contents

Acknowledgements

With thanks to my family and friends for their help and inspiration, especially the late Kathleen Preston who knew the Boggarts well.

For Ruby

TINSEL TOWER
BEWARE OF
BUZZ OFF!
TEMPORARY PALACE
THE RIVER WYRM
TWEEDLE DALE MODERN HOUSING ESTATE
HERE THERE BE BOGGARTS

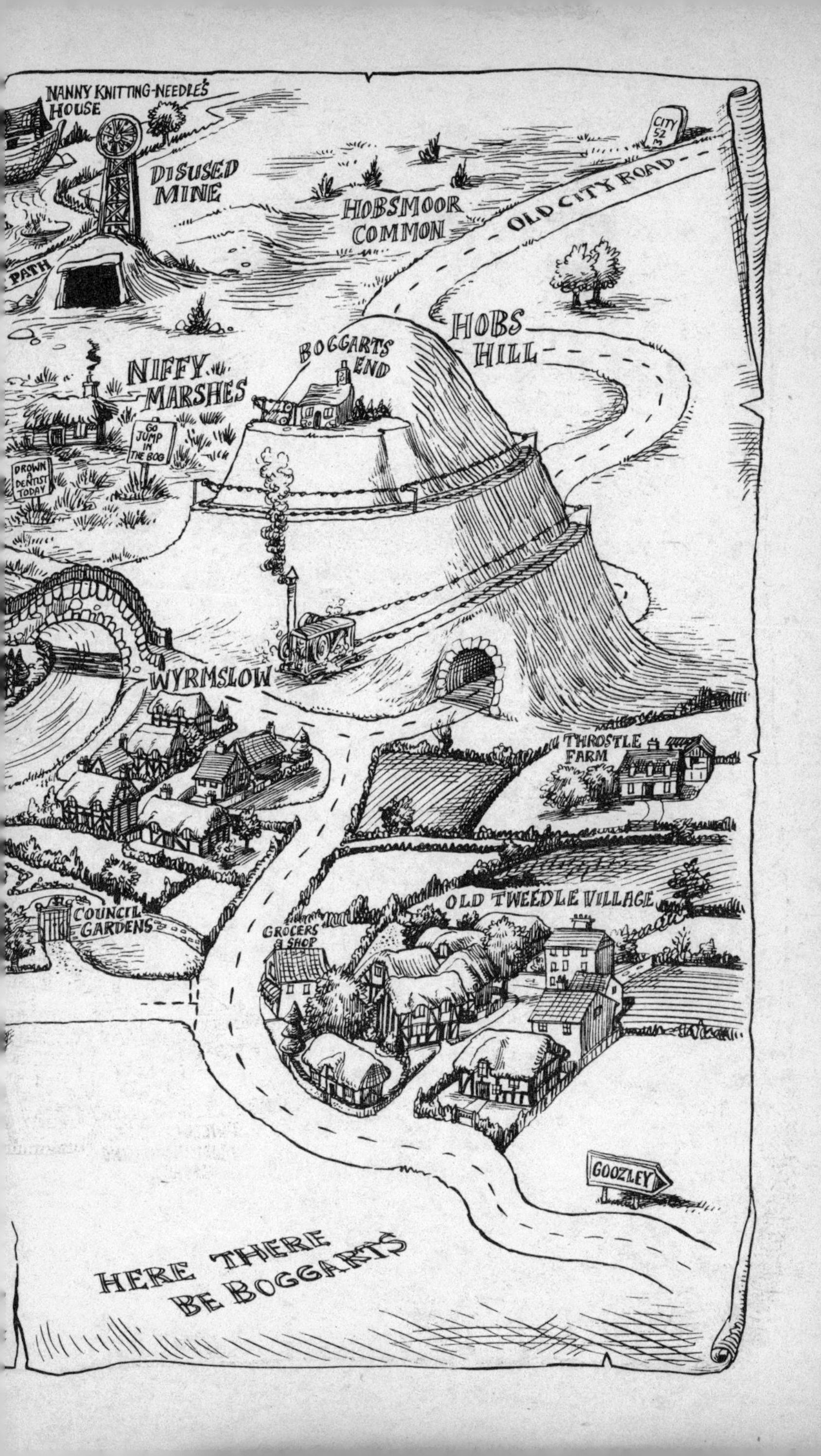
NANNY KNITTING-NEEDLE'S HOUSE
DISUSED MINE
HOBSMOOR COMMON
CITY 52 M
OLD CITY ROAD
PATH
HOBS HILL
BOGGARTS END
NIFFY MARSHES
GO JUMP IN THE BOG
DROWN A DENTIST TODAY
WYRMSLOW
THROSTLE FARM
OLD TWEEDLE VILLAGE
GROCERS SHOP
COUNCIL GARDENS
GOOZLEY
HERE THERE BE BOGGARTS

Song of the Midsummer Boggarts

Scritching by the fireside, a shadow on the wall,
Thunder in the bogle-hole behind the waterfall,
Laughter from an empty barn, dancing faery lights,
Echoes from the hillside on wild midsummer-nights!
Out come all we Boggartyboos to play!
Why does everybody run away?

chorus Boggarty Boggarty Boo!
We want to be friends with you!
Wild and Witchery,
Tricksy, Twitchery,
Hairy, Tattery,
Mad as a Hattery,
Boggarty Boggarty Boo!

A rustle in the rushes, a cackle in your ear,
Something splishy splashy in the misty murky mere,
Something gone that wasn't there, nothing to be
seen,
Just a row of smiling teeth, each one mossy-green.
Out come all we Boggartyboos to play!
Why does everybody run away?

Howling down your chimney! Tapping on your
door!
Underneath your armchair! Underneath your floor!
Munching in your kitchen! Prancing down your
street!
What a shame the likes of you and us so seldom
meet!
Out come all we Boggartyboos to play!
Why does everybody run away?

The Waterboggart Picnic Song

I'd swim a million miles or more
Through an inky stinky sewerpipe for
Some duckweed jelly and watersnail pie,
– Rat's-tail soup with dragonfly!

chorus So pick up your spoon and slurp!
Pat your tummy and burp!
Flap your feet while you sing along
With the Waterboggart Picnic Song!

I'd cross an ocean and back again
Sailing on the back of an old moorhen
For a frogspawn pudding going nicely brown.
– Pondslime tea to wash it down!

I'd dive to the bottom of the deep dark sea
With a shoal of sharks all after me
For a toadspit sarni with fisheye sauce!
– Sludgecake for my second course!

I'd whirl in a whirlpool round and round,
Up in a waterspout off the ground
For the tastiest treat in the picnic box,
– Crunchy water beetle chocs!

Introduction

Boggart rhymes with yoghurt, and the stress is the same. (Unless you're one of those strange people who call yoghurt '*yoh*-gurt', in which case Boggart rhymes with dogdirt.)

Boggarts are generally smaller than us. They come in a range of sizes and shapes, but are never as small, or as well dressed, as pixies or fairies. (As a matter of fact, many Boggarts don't believe in fairies.) If you met a Boggart off-duty you might imagine you'd seen a small, strangely dressed, odd looking person – but if you met Jack Ironteeth grinning at you down a deep hole, or Jinny Greenteeth rising out of a swamp . . . you'd probably just go 'Aaaargh!'

All Boggarts are related to the Common Tattery Boggart. They avoid looking smart, and well dressed, apart from Hob Headless, and are easily insulted, especially by offers of new clothes, or a wash and tidy. They're quick to change their moods – noisy, proud, loud and boastful, silent and sulky, loving, enthusiastic, sentimental, and over-excited. They have a tendency to talk all together all at once when they're trying to discuss something, and in general are more like us than we are ourselves.

Boggarts are elemental creatures, and have special and magical qualities according to their kind. They can all manage to be invisible sometimes – though some find it easier than others.

Boggarts like Bloodnose Redcap have a wild time in wild places, but others may be equally at home lounging unseen by your fireside, like Waggat'wa or Hob-Lie-By-The-Fire.

Boggarts live at the edge of our lives. Perhaps you'd like to know them better . . .

Tale 1

JINNY GREENTEETH and the TRAVELLING DENTIST

The moon shone full and fat and high on Hobsmoor Common. It lit up every leafy dip and hollow. It beamed into every badger's den and rabbit's burrow.

But there was one dark hole too deep by far, even for the moon's wide eye.

And out of that hole in the ground that night came a fearful whirring and whizzing, a grinding and clanging – and the whine of a drill, a high-power drill, screeching away in the echoing deep.

Hobsmoor Coal Mine had been closed for hundreds of years, but some said there was a Boggart down there, a Mining Boggart with a luminous grin called Jack Ironteeth, who lived at the bottom of the old pit shaft.

The drill gave one last scream and died, but the silence was soon broken . . . this time by a spluttering fizzing sound, as the underground cave crackled with lightning, a sudden flashing and sparking – far brighter than the moon.

It was the dentist.

It was Painless Percy Simmonds – Travelling Dentist, who was fixing Jack's teeth with a spot of painless welding.

Jack Ironteeth didn't get plaque or dental decay but he suffered from rust and his metal molars were badly dented from chewing lumps of coal.

While he worked with his welding torch, Percy chattered away to his patient.

'How's life, then? Been on your holidays lately? Frightened any pot-holers?'

Of course there was no reply to any of these questions because Jack's mouth was full of welding rod. All he could say was, 'Oooo er ahh worh waaa'. But Percy wasn't bothered – it gave him more

chance to talk about himself.

'I was doing a deep filling on a dragon last week, nearly burnt me socks off! 'Course I was wearing my fire-fighting suit so there wasn't too much damage. At least you can see what you're doing with a big beast. I had a leprechaun in the chair once, six inches high, and wouldn't sit still. Wriggling all the time he was, an' wouldn't have gas in case I stole his crock of gold while he was asleep! Griffins are the worst. One turned me into a toad once – said I gave her an earache, but I never touched her ears!'

Jack Ironteeth didn't mind the blathering. He even put up with the smell of Percy's aftershave, because that was the nastiest thing Painless Percy ever made his patients suffer. After his teeth had been finished off with wire wool and metal polish, Jack paid Percy his highest compliment.

'Not bad, Mr Simmonds . . . not bad at all!'

Percy accepted the compliment and the cup of tea that went with it.

'Where are you off to now?' asked Jack.

'Wyrmslow Village Cemetery. I've got a vampire to see before the dawn breaks.'

'Be careful!'

'No need, Jack. He's a vegetarian – he just drinks too much Cherry Cola for his tooth enamel!'

'I don't mean be careful of *him*, Mr Simmonds! I mean, *be careful how you go!* I'd avoid Niffy Marshes if I were you!'

'But it's the quickest way, and there's a full moon tonight so I won't fall in the mire.'

'You might not *fall* in, Mr Simmonds, but Jinny Greenteeth might *drag* you in! She's a Swamp Boggart and she's got a thing about dentists!'

Percy Simmonds had never heard of Jinny Greenteeth, which was surprising because he fancied he knew everybody. He must have decided that Jack was having him on, because as soon as he'd climbed out of the old mineshaft he set a straight course for Wyrmslow Village, right across Niffy Marshes.

The moon was low in the sky now, and looming even larger behind the twisty trees. As Percy followed the path that wound between the river and the marsh, a brown owl flew from branch to branch along the way, turning each time to hoot at him till he caught up.

Percy was inspired to sing:

'I'm Painless Percy Simmonds
The Travelling Dentist-o!
The Moon is my Lantern in the Sky!
An Owl is my Guide below!'

So taken was Percy with his song and the owl and the moon, that he didn't notice he'd wandered off the path into the reedy marshland, and he didn't notice a long green arm snaking out between the rushes – not until it was too late, not until a scabby green hand had grabbed him by the ankle, snatched his legs from under him, and pulled him into the morass!

'Help!' cried Percy as he felt himself being dragged deeper and deeper into the swamp. But the only answer was the hoot of the owl as it flew off across the moon, and a nasty gurgling laugh in his left ear.

Percy turned and saw a thin puce-green face, with snot-green eyes, and slime-green hair. The mouth was wide open, revealing two rows of moss-green teeth.

Percy Simmonds thought his dental days were over, but he was a true professional to the last. Even as he sank deeper into the murky mire he noticed something seriously amiss in Jinny Greenteeth's mouth.

'Aha!' he exclaimed. 'Buccal Occlusal!'

'You what?' cried Jinny, opening her mouth even wider. 'Nobody speaks to me like that!'

'Lower left seven. . . . Deep cavity. . . . Buccal Occlusal! It means there's a big hole in one of your back teeth!' explained Percy. 'It must be giving you gyp!'

'A dentist! I *hate* dentists!' shrieked Jinny Greenteeth. 'Now you're really for it! I've just invented a special torture especially for dentists!'

With that she grabbed hold of him by the neck, pulled him out of the bog like a cork out of a bottle, and dragged him after her into the misty middle of Niffy Marshes.

'I'm going to cover you with something unspeakably slimy, hang you by your feet over a slow burning fire, roll you in the nettles and feed you to the alligators!'

'There aren't any alligators in Niffy Marshes,' thought Percy, hopefully.

'And don't worry if we can't find any alligators!' said Jinny. 'I'll chop you up fine and feed you to the tadpoles if I have to, you . . . you . . . you . . . Dentist!!!'

By now they had arrived at a little wooden hut on stilts with a variety of friendly notices pinned over the door, saying things like 'Drown a Dentist Today!' and 'Go Jump in the Bog!'.

Percy didn't really want to go inside, but Jinny was too strong for him. She pushed him into her kitchen, threw some logs on the fire and began scraping up some furry green potato salad that was oozing its way out of the larder.

'It's last year's,' said Jinny as she trussed Percy up like a chicken and began spreading it over him. 'I've been saving it for a special occasion.'

'You really mean what you say, don't you?' wailed Percy. 'Why do you hate dentists so much?'

'You know why!' said Jinny. 'They torture people, so I torture them back! There's no such thing as painless dentists, only lying dentists. They say things like, "This won't hurt at all", and then they ram things in your mouth and attack you with drills! Only *I'm* never gonna be tortured by a dentist 'cos I won't let one near me. What I'm tortured by is *toothache*, and it's *all your fault*!'

By now Jinny had finished spreading him with rotten potato salad and was hoisting him upside down over the open fire.

'Wait a bit!' coughed Percy, 'I've got it! You're *afraid* of dentists!'

'You must be joking!' said Jinny, and then sat down by the fire and burst into tears.

Percy was beginning to smoulder. 'Don't cry. Don't cry!' he said. 'I can help you! Cut me down before it's too late! Do you want that toothache for ever?'

Jinny Greenteeth considered for a moment, but didn't cut him down. 'I'll give you a try,' she said, 'but if you torture me one little bit I'll do something back to you that makes dangling over the fire seem like a birthday treat!!'

Percy didn't ask what that might be. 'Anything! Anything you say! Quick, before I go crispy! . . . Yaaaaaaaaaaa!'

After Jinny had thrown a jug of stagnant water over him, Percy was ready for action again. Jinny rescued his bag from the bottom of Niffy Marshes and he did his best to clean and sterilise his dental instruments on the kitchen table.

Jinny sat in her armchair twitching nervously. 'Don't you dare come anywhere near me with those things!'

'I'll have to eventually,' said Percy. 'They're for fixing your teeth. But you won't feel anything because I'll give you something to make you go numb.'

'Like a smack on the head?'

'No. Just a little injection with this needle. . . . Say Ah!'

But Jinny didn't say 'Ah!' She said, 'Not on your life, buster!' snatched the needle out of Percy's hand and stuck it straight into his backside.

Percy gave a terrible shriek of pain, charged out of the door, ran three times round Jinny's hut, and was still hopping from one foot to another when he ran back in again.

'We'll have to call you "Painful Percy with the Numb Bum",' laughed Jinny! 'I thought you said it wouldn't hurt.'

'It wouldn't have!' groaned Percy. 'I was going to do it very carefully.'

Jinny put her long green nose right up against Percy's little round white nose, and stared him right in both his eyes.

'I don't like needles,' she said determinedly.

Percy didn't argue. He reached into his bag and pulled out a metal cylinder. 'We'll try gas and air,' he said. 'It comes through this tube and out of this mask. It'll make you feel sort of floaty.'

Jinny sat by Percy and took a few breaths through the mask. Her face seemed to be going an even more horrible shade of green than normal.

'I don't feel sort of floaty, Mister Painless Percy! I feel sort of sick!!'

'It's not supposed to do that!' said Percy.

'It's not the gas that's making me feel sick,' said Jinny. 'And it's not the mouldy potato salad. It's something much more smelly than that.'

'What's that?' asked Percy.

'Your aftershave!' gurgled Jinny.

Percy gave up on the gas and air, but he had one more trick up his sleeve – hypnotism! He sat Jinny on her kitchen chair and dangled his watch in front of her eyes.

'You are going into a deep sleep,' said Percy in a sing-song voice.

'I am going into a deep sleep,' moaned Jinny Greenteeth.

'I am going to fill your tooth and you won't feel a thing,' chanted Percy.

'I won't feel a thing,' moaned Jinny. 'And if you don't take that metal thing out of my mouth, I'll bite your head off!'

Then she leapt out of the chair and threw Percy through the window onto a very old compost heap. Percy was really smelly now, and really frightened too, but Jinny didn't bite his head off. She came out of the door and said something quite unexpected.

'I don't mind a bit of pain, you know, not if it means I get rid of the toothache.'

'Well what's all the fuss about then?' said Percy from the compost.

'It's just that I don't like people doing things in my mouth, without they tell me exactly what it is they're doing.'

'Really! Really! That's easy,' said Percy. 'Let's go inside and start again.'

'Not till I've cleaned you up a bit,' said Jinny, turning a hosepipe on him. 'I don't mind the smell of compost, but I can't take any more of your disgusting aftershave!'

Jinny wrapped Percy in an old towel while his clothes were drying, and suggested he start again. Percy held up a shiny instrument.

'I'm just going to put this in your mouth . . .'

'What is it?' asked Jinny.

'It's a mirror and probe,' said Percy.

'What's it for?' asked Jinny.

'For seeing if there's any decay in that tooth at the back,' said Percy.

'What exactly is decay?' asked Jinny.

'We dentists call it dental caries,' said Percy '. . . Look! You'll have to trust me! I can't tell you everything or I'll end up giving you a dental training course.'

'Suits me!' said Jinny Greenteeth.

'All right!' said Percy, 'But you'll have to come on my rounds with me. I've got plenty of other patients to attend to besides you.'

They just made it to Wyrmslow Churchyard in time

to fit the vampire's crumbling right fang with a large pointed gold crown. Afterwards Jinny Greenteeth followed Percy round on the rest of his dental travels.

She learned about high-speed drills, and suction tubes for keeping the mouth dry. She learned how to fill teeth with amalgam pluggers, and how to use a wards carver for making the filling fit the chew. ('It's called the *bite*!' said Percy, 'Not the *chew*!') She learned how to use a round-end burnisher, and a pear-shaped burnisher. She learned the proper way to brush and floss so you don't need so many fillings in the first place.

Eventually she knew so much that she was examined by the Royal College of Dental Surgeons and awarded her Royal Dental Certificate.

By this time she'd let Percy fill her bad tooth, and although the rest of her molars were still naturally green, they weren't full of plaque and decay.

The year had come full circle, and Percy and Jinny had arrived at the bottom of the darkest hole on Hobsmoor.

'I told you not to take that short cut!' said Jack, when Percy finally took the welder out of his mouth. 'Now look where it's got you. She'll be wanting a partnership next!'

'Aaaagh!' screamed Percy.

'What's so bad about that?' snapped Jinny. 'I do half the work already! We'll call ourselves "Simmonds and Greenteeth – The Famous Swampland Dental Practice (strange and difficult patients a speciality)"!'

'Aaaagh! It's not that!' cried Percy. 'It's my tooth!'

'Come over here,' said Jinny, taking Percy by the arm and leading him towards a large armchair. 'Sit down here, and let me have a look at it!'

'No. It's no bother,' whimpered Percy, trying to pull out of her grasp. 'It'll wait!'

'No it won't!'

'It will! It'll wait.'

'That's odd!' said Jack Ironteeth. 'You're usually dead keen to get teeth seen to – when they're other people's!'

Percy was looking a bit pale now. He was biting his bottom lip and twiddling his fingers together nervously. 'Got to go now,' he said. 'Other patients to see.'

'Wait a bit!' gasped Jinny Greenteeth. 'You're not . . . ? You are! You're . . .'

'Yes, I am . . . slightly afraid of dentists!' sighed Percy Painless Simmonds, as he gave up the struggle, lay back in the armchair and opened his mouth.

'Nice and wide, please!' said Jinny Greenteeth. 'Nice and wide!'

Tale 2

BOGGART SANDWICH and NOTHING ELSE

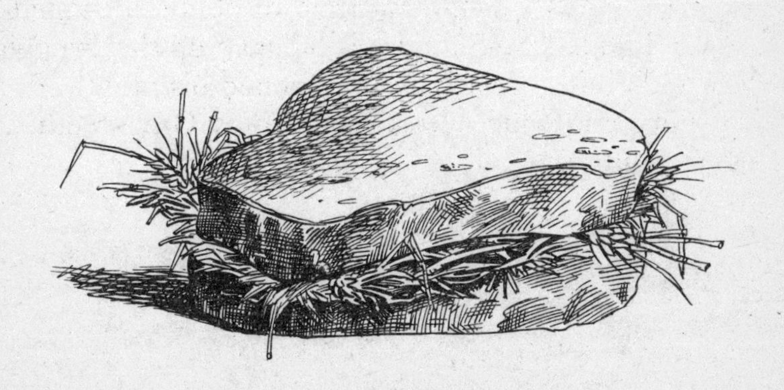

The summer sun rose early and shone brightly on Tweedledale Modern Housing Estate for the comfortably well off. Tweedledale was full of big new houses, all of them wishing they felt as comfortable as the little cottages in Old Tweedle Village.

The sun twinkled on their coach lamps, sparkled on the bobbly glass of their big bay windows, bounced off the bonnets of their smart cars, and glinted smugly on one or two private swimming pools.

Only when it came to Willow Lodge, otherwise known as No. 3 Tweedley Dean, did the sun lose its confidence. Fiffi ffarh-Headingley was only just crawling out of her bed, and there was no point in beaming like a Smiley Badge till Fiffi decided what mood she was in.

Fiffi's parents, Peter and Rita ffarh-Headingley, felt the same way. They knew they had to give Fiffi *everything* she wanted, *when* she wanted it, exactly *how* she wanted it or suffer the consequences.

Breakfast-time was terrifying. Fiffi made the rules, and Fiffi could change the rules. You only had to give her the wrong spoon, or the cup without the rabbits on, and the sun wouldn't shine all day.

Peter and Rita ffarh-Headingley held their breath as Fiffi ran downstairs, still wearing her Cuddlyfun Cutiebear pyjamas, and sat at the table.

It was the right seat. So far so good!

And the knife was the right knife – not the little one she could handle easily, but the big heavy one she liked to keep dropping.

Rita picked it off the floor a couple of times and then trembled a little as Fiffi grabbed her soldiers of toast and peered at them closely.

It looked like trouble. But no – the toast was still warm, and the butter had been spread (not too thick, not too thin) to the very edge of each individual slice.

Not only that, Fiffi's boiled egg (chopped clean across the top with a knife, and never messily smashed on the head with a spoon) had just the right softness of yolk, and a hard white without any dribbly glucky yuch.

Just as she finished the last mouthful the sun decided it was safe to carry on shining.

Peter decided he could read the paper before he left for work at the advertising agency.

Rita decided to plan the dance class she ran on Tuesday afternoons.

And then it was Fiffi's turn to decide.

'. . . I want some beans.'

Fiffi's father froze in the middle of the sports page, threw his paper into the air, and ran to the kitchen. 'I'll get you some. I'll get you some right away!'

'Your father's getting you some,' repeated Rita nervously.

'I want some beans *now*!' whined Fiffi.

'Yes, now, right away, right now. Daddy will be heating them up right now!'

No he wasn't. Daddy was running very fast into the little grocer's shop in Old Tweedle Village. He arrived all hot-pink-and-breathless, and pushed to the front of the queue, elbowing aside Mrs Halibutt-Discovery-Fortesque who would never speak to him again.

'I'm sorry! I'm sorry! It's an emergency. Beans – any beans – quickly!'

Back indoors the temperature was rising.

'*Mummeeeee* . . . Where's my *beans*!'

'They're coming!'

'I'm *hungreeeee*!'

'You can't be that hungry. You've just eaten your breakfast.'

That was where Rita was mistaken. . . .

'I can be as hungry as I want to be!' declared Fiffi, and then, after a slight sniff and a moan, 'I'm *starving* hungry 'cos you don't give me enough to eat, and I'm going to tell my *Granny from Goozley*!'

Rita screamed and ran into the kitchen. 'Peter! The beans! Quickly!'

Peter wasn't there, but Rita could see him legging it down the lane. She flung open the kitchen window and yelled out to him. 'The beans! The beans!'

Peter leapt over the fence, and threw the beans through the window. Rita caught them, opened the tin with her magno-electric opener, threw the beans into a bowl, threw the bowl into the microwave, waited for the bleep, then ran with the bowl into the breakfast room.

She felt like throwing the beans at Fiffi, but she put them down in front of her and said, 'There you are, nice hot beans in your bowl with the little ponies round the edge.'

Fiffi should have been happy, but somehow she looked a bit peeved. 'I want to eat them with a spoon! My birthday spoon with the red handle!'

Rita pulled it out from behind her back. 'I thought you would!'

Fiffi looked even more peeved.

'Come on then!' said Peter. 'Eat your nice beans. . . . I thought you were hungry!'

Fiffi sulkily spooned a few beans up to her lips . . . and then spat them out!

'Euuugh!' she cried, throwing her tomato saucy spoon onto the clean tablecloth. 'These are Foggarty's Happyface Funbeans! I wanted Finnigans Sillyface Fatbeans!'

The sun went and hid behind a cloud.

'Whatever the boss says!' groaned Peter.

Fiffi thought he might be making fun of her, so she started to cry. 'Waaaaaa! I don't want beans anymore!'

'What *do* you want?' asked Rita.

Fiffi wasn't sure yet but her performance was in full swing. The crying got louder and louder until it turned into a screaming fit. The screaming fit turned into a throwing fit – and once she'd broken her cup with the bunnies and chipped her bowl with the ponies, there was no turning back.

'You never let me have what I want!' she shouted. 'I hate you and I'm going to hold my breath now till I choke!'

Fiffi went red, and then blue, and then purple,

while Peter and Rita jumped up and down and pulled their hair out.

'You can have anything you like!' cried Peter.

'Yes, anything!' insisted Rita.

Fiffi took a deep breath, wiped her eyes, and sat on her favourite chair. 'Anything . . . you promised.'

'Well, yes, within reason,' mumbled Peter pitifully.

Fiffi looked him in the eye. 'Granny from Goozley says it's the wickedest thing in the world to break a promise to a little child.'

Rita noticed that Fiffi was looking at the telephone. 'We promised and we meant it!' she said quickly.

'Sugar-toasted Honeycrunch Munchflakes,' said Fiffi.

Munchflakes were sent for, and Munchflakes arrived.

Fiffi tasted the Munchflakes. 'Too soggy!'

'But they're Honeycrunch Munchflakes!' gasped Peter. 'Cuddlyfun Cutiebears love them! Yum, yum, yum!'

'Cuddlyfun Cutiebears detest them! Yeuch, yeuch, yeuch!' shouted Fiffi. 'You promised I could have what I like, and now you won't let meeeee!'

Peter telephoned the office to say he might be late.

Fiffi had an inspiration. 'Kippers!'

'You hate kippers!' said Rita.

'I want to see if I still hate them as much!' said Fiffi.

Peter came back with best Aberdeen kippers from the fishmongers in town and Fiffi found that she hated them just as much as she ever did. Next door's

cat, Jubilee, had the mid-morning snack of a lifetime, and then Fiffi went into top gear.

'I want Spaghetti Bolognese, Peking Spare Ribs, and Curried Spinach and Potato!'

Peter had just come from town, so he slumped on the sofa while Rita trailed round Mario's Italian restaurant, the Sang Sang Chinese, and the Tandoori.

While she was away Fiffi made her father read to her out of *The Blue Ribbon Guide to Posh Nosh for Top Toffs*. There were so many descriptions and full-colour pictures of mouth-watering and expensive dishes that by the time all her meals had arrived Fiffi had completely changed her mind.

Peter and Rita ate the take-aways for their lunch, Peter phoned his office to say he wouldn't be in at all that day, Rita cancelled her dance class – and Fiffi gave out her latest orders.

'I want Raw Shark and Lobster Eggs, Oysters with Caviar and Champagne Sauce, followed by Kiwi Sorbet with Fresh Guava!'

'No . . . no . . .' moaned Peter and Rita.

'Yes . . . yes . . .' screamed Fiffi. 'Or I'll tell Granny from Goozley on you!'

Peter drove off to the distant city to fetch the special food and a special cook to cook it.

Fiffi wouldn't play. She wouldn't sleep. She wouldn't listen to stories. All she would do was scream all the time and threaten to phone her Granny from Goozley if they didn't bring her just what she liked.

Next morning Peter came back with a chef dressed all in white with a special hat. The chef spent six hours in the kitchen, with Peter and Rita to help him, and finally the special meal was served up to Fiffi on a special silver plate, on a special white tablecloth, with special flowers and candles.

The chef stood proudly and waited. Fiffi tasted it and said it tasted about as special as old socks in cat sick.

The chef shouted a lot of words in French before he left, but Fiffi didn't care. She'd found another book called *The Galloping World Explorers' Guide To Far-out Food*!

Peter phoned the office to say he wouldn't be in for the rest of the week. He was flying to Australia, to find some live witchetty grubs.

Fiffi thought the witchetty grubs were quite nice, but didn't like the way they wiggled in her mouth.

Rita went on safari to hunt aardvark in Africa.

Fiffi thought it tasted too much like cold spam fritters.

Peter came back from South America with an alligator.

Fiffi decided to keep it as a pet and let it swim in her Cuddlyfun Cutiebear paddling pool.

The house filled up with rejected food, but nothing they found would please her.

Peter telephoned work to say he wouldn't be in next week either and his boss told him not to bother coming back ever.

'We've spent all our money trying to please you,' said Rita. 'You've got to eat something, Fiffi!'

'There's *nothing* I've got to do!' cried Fiffi. 'It's up to you to find me what I like, or I'll phone Granny!'

Fiffi's parents had finally had enough. 'Go on then!' said Peter, thrusting the phone at her. 'See if we care! Phone your Granny from Goozley, and tell her just how badly we treat you!'

Fiffi snatched the phone, but before she could dial a number the front door flew open.

'Granny's here!' announced a strong clear voice from the hall.

There was a rustling and bustling, and then into the room swept a short, slightly dumpy figure, dressed in a long yellow tweed frock, a yellow cape, yellow boots and green hat with what looked like a bundle of dry grass tied to it for decoration.

'You're not my Granny from Goozley!' gasped Fiffi.

'No!' said the Granny. 'I'm your Granny from Wyrmslow.'

'I didn't know I had a Granny from Wyrmslow,' said Fiffi.

'We didn't know you had a Granny from Wyrmslow,' said Peter and Rita.

'Well, you know now,' said the Granny. 'I've just come to warn you that if you carry on like this Hobthross will get you!'

'What's Hobthross?' said Fiffi defiantly.

'Hobthross is a Boggart . . . a magical Boggart who knows how to deal with a fusspot!' said Granny.

Fiffi didn't care for being talked to like this. 'I'm

not frightened of Boggarts or any other creature!' she shouted defiantly. 'I'll have it in a sandwich!'

Fiffi was mightily pleased at her own cleverness. 'Yes, that's what I'd like to eat – Boggart Sandwich and nothing else!'

'That's easily arranged,' said Granny from Wyrmslow. 'I happen to have brought some Hobthross sandwiches with me.'

'I won't finish them if I don't like them,' said Fiffi suspiciously.

'Oh, you'll like them!' said Granny from Wyrmslow, taking some sandwiches from her pocket and handing one over.

Fiffi sniffed at it and gave it a little nibble. It was delicious . . . like nothing else she'd ever tasted. She gave it a big bite, then crammed it into her mouth, and reached for another one, and then . . . and then she stopped . . . with open mouth and eyes wide.

'Something wrong?' said Granny from Wyrmslow. 'You'll appreciate, of course, that Hobthross is a Straw Boggart.'

Fiffi hadn't appreciated it, but she did now because the sandwich had turned to straw in her mouth. She ran to get a glass of water to wash it out . . . but the water turned to straw as well.

Fiffi was terrified, but she couldn't speak for the straw. Peter and Rita were frightened too.

'Don't worry,' said Granny. 'There's always a cure for a Hobthross Boggart Sandwich, but she'll have to try all the food round here till she finds it.'

It took hours. It wasn't aardvark. It wasn't witchetty grubs. It wasn't lobster eggs or champagne sauce. Every kind of food and drink turned to straw in her mouth until there was nothing left to try. Fiffi sat at the table with tears rolling down her cheeks. Peter and Rita gave her a hug and tried to comfort her.

'I think she's learned her lesson now,' said Rita.

'She may have,' said Granny, 'but have you?'

'Yes, I'm sure we have,' said Peter. 'Tell us what the cure is.'

'It can't be in this house!' said Rita. 'We've tried everything!'

'Not quite everything . . .' said Granny from Wyrmslow, and looked across to the windowsill where the sun shone confidently on a chipped bowl with ponies round the edge – containing quite a few baked beans.

They were Foggarty's Happyface Funbeans, now very cold and very old!

Tale 3

The Boggart Who Wouldn't Tell Her Name

It was a damp drizzly day, in a wild and soggy place on the River Wyrm. The grassy river bank squelched underfoot as Nanny Knitting Needles frogmarched her four grandchildren down to the water's edge.

'Mind how you go, my loves! It's not a race! Ruth! Beth! Seth! Careful with that picnic box! Wake up, Luke!'

A wet and clammy granny Nanny was! A Waterboggart she was, with webskin spread wide between fingers and toes, and eyes like dark swirls in the deep river.

'All aboard, my loves! Come along, Luke – you'll be left behind!' Nanny hustled her grandchildren onto a wooden raft, and set off upstream.

Beth, Seth, Ruth and Luke sat at the back, kicking the craft through the water with their webbed feet. Nanny Knitting Needles sat up front on the picnic box . . . and knitted the river.

Whirlpools and eddies she knitted,
Rocks and weeds,
Plain water and pearl water,
Greens, blues, and greys!

She wove in the wobbly reflection of a tree, and dropped a stitch for an occasional sunbeam.

When it felt like lunchtime they beached their boat on a comfortable-looking island, and sang the Waterboggart Picnic Song:

'I'd swim a million miles or more
Through an inky stinky sewerpipe for
Some duckweed jelly and watersnail pie,
Rat's-tail soup with dragonfly. . . . !'

They were about to belt out another finger-licking

verse, featuring pondslime and frogspawn, when they were interrupted by an earthquake. The ground, the trees, the Boggarts' knees . . . everything wobbled at once as the world filled up with a hideous, thunderous, eardrum-cracking shout!

Nanny's first thought was that the earth-shaking yell had come from Gizzit Blubbergut Munch, a Monstrous Ogre who had just appeared, towering above the trees, on the opposite bank of the river.

Then it happened again! 'Yarararooraraaaaah!'

And Nanny saw that the noise had nothing to do with the Monstrous Ogre – who had his monstrous fingers in his monstrous ears, and his monstrous mouth shut tight.

'Well, what's making all the racket?!' she demanded.

Luke pointed to the far shore. 'Look! Loooook! S'aboggart!'

There on the reedy riverside edge, facing the advancing ogre with her back to the water, was a wild Boggart – not a Waterboggart or a Common Tattery Boggart, but a kind of Boggart they'd never seen before. She was small but broad-shouldered – and she couldn't half shout!

'Yarararooraraaaaah!'

Once again the world trembled, but the Monstrous Ogre stuck his monstrous fingers even more firmly in his monstrous ears, and stomped towards her.

'Dive in and swim for it!' shouted Ruth.

'She can't swim or she'd be in by now,' said Luke.

'Blubbergut Munch'll have her for Lunch!' chanted Beth and Seth.

Nanny didn't think it was time for silly rhymes.

She pulled out four spare pairs of fat 00 gauge knitting needles and chucked them at her grandchildren. 'That's enough chitter chatter! Let's save her life!'

Catching the needles, quickly they set to work! A busy click-clacking began then as all five Waterboggarts all-together knitted the river.

They knitted it rough. They stitched it up and around.
They knitted a troublesome bubblesome merry-go-round.
They wove the water to fume and froth and fly,
Then cast it helter-skelter up to the sky!

Gizzit Blubbergut Munch stopped dead in his giant tracks as he saw a great whirling waterspout rise out of the river and snake up to the clouds above his head. 'It's a bit like water being sucked down a plughole,' he thought, 'only the other way up!'

Then there wasn't time for any more giant thoughts. The rushing column of water twisted towards him, caught him by an arm and a leg, wooshed him topsy-turvy, twizzled him into a blur of colour and cries for help . . . and then tossed the terrified ogre into the air!

The Boggarts watched him, bouncing around like a ping-pong ball on top of the waterspout, as it carried him away down the River Wyrm to the distant sea.

Nanny and her grandchildren put away their knitting needles, and paddled across to rescue the young Boggart with the loud voice. Now it was all over she just stood there in silence.

Beth, Seth, and Ruth had plenty to say. 'Did y'see that flying giant! We stitched him up alright!' 'How did you do that earthquake shout?' 'Yeah! Do it again!'

'Leave her alone,' said Luke.

'That's right!' said Nanny. 'Now then, little one . . . what's your name?'

There was no reply. Nanny tried a different tack. 'Where's your mother and father?'

More silence.

'Did the Monstrous Ogre get them?'

A nod . . .

There were no more questions! Nanny scooped her up and sat her on the raft. 'Beth! Seth! Ruth! Wake up Luke, and get paddling! We're taking this one home to live with us!'

That was the kind of Boggart Nanny was!

Later that evening, Nanny and her grandchildren sat round the tea table with the new member of the family.

'She's not eaten her snail pie,' said Ruth. 'And she's left pondslime on the plate.'

'If you won't eat the stew, there's no pudding for you!' chanted Seth and Beth together.

'Leave her alone,' said Luke.

'That's all you ever say!' taunted Ruth.

'Quiet, both of you!' said Nanny. 'This Boggart's just had her mum and dad eaten by an ogre!' Then she turned to the orphan with a smile. 'Now then, little one, you haven't uttered one word since you arrived. What's your name?'

'None of your business!'

Beth, Seth, Ruth, Luke fell off their chairs. Nobody had ever spoken like that to their grandmother.

'And didn't we just save you from an ogre?!' gasped Nanny Knitting Needles.

'I'm a Thunderboggart,' announced the newcomer. 'I don't eat pondslime! I eat crab apples and I've got a magic loud voice.'

'We know that!' said Ruth. 'And I'm a Waterboggart, so if you don't tell us your name I'll knit a whirlpool and drown you in it!'

'If I told people my name I wouldn't have a magic loud voice any more! It'd zip zap zoom and vanish away.'

''Course it wouldn't,' said Nanny.

'That's a stupid idea!' said Beth.

'It's not stupid!' screamed the Thunderboggart. 'It's true! You're not my mum anyway, and I'm not telling you anything, so shut up!'

That was her last word. No amount of kindness or cajoling made any difference so they had to live with a nameless Boggart.

Sometimes they called her 'Thingummy!' Sometimes 'Hey you!' or 'What's-yer-name?'

Sometimes Nanny's grandchildren invented names like 'Smellydrainbreath' or 'Cowpatface' to try and taunt her into speaking.

Luke was the only one who didn't fuss or bother. When the others had given up he'd go and sit beside her. He was so quiet she didn't even notice he was there.

All the neighbours had heard about the Thunderboggart by now. They kept popping round to have a peek at her.

'Hello, Nanny!' they'd say. 'How's your new . . ., you know, . . . er, Little Miss Nobody with the big mouth?'

Soon the story spread throughout the land – the story of a Thunderboggart who could use her voice to make the ground shake, but wouldn't even whisper her name in Nanny's ear.

'She saved that girl from being eaten by an ogre! . . . And now she can't get two words out of her!'

'It's a shame. That's what I call it. A crying shame!'

Horris Waggat'wa, Temporary King of The Boggarts at the time, hearing this tittle-tattle underneath his kitchen window, stuck his head out to ask if the gossip had anything to do with a

Monstrous Ogre he'd once seen flying out to sea on a waterspout.

The gossipers told him it certainly had, and a lot more besides. The King 'ooo'd' and 'ahhhh'd' and 'ooo'd' again as he listened to their story.

Horris suffered from insatiable curiosity, and now he couldn't rest till he'd heard the magic loud voice for himself.

'Bring her here! Summon her to the palace! If she'll speak to anyone at all, she'll surely speak to the Temporary King of The Boggarts!'

Three days later a messenger brought a terrible panic to Nanny's riverside residence.

'Now then, my little mystery!' said Nanny, waving the royal invitation. 'Are you going to disgrace us all or are you going to get that tongue unglued for His Majesty?'

On the day of the Special Reception the Temporary Palace was squashed full of Boggarts, Boggarts of the Clouds and Mountains, Boggarts of Back Gardens and Airing Cupboards, all shapes of Boggart, talking and arguing at once, as is their custom.

Horris sat in the middle of the hubbub, his floppy ears sticking out from under his temporary crown, trying hard to hear what was going on.

And then the King's herald, the silvery-skinned Killmoulis, trumpeted an alarm through his funnel-mouth. After a few minutes' confusion a space was cleared before the throne, and into it walked a slightly embarrassed Nanny Knitting Needles. She had a little Thunderboggart grasped in one hand,

three over-excited grandchildren running ahead, and Luke trailing behind as usual.

King Waggat'wa made them repeat the story six times from everybody's point of view. By the end of this, some of the fidgety Boggarts were sucking their thumbs and others picking the cheesy bits between their toes.

Hob-Lie-By-The-Fire lost patience. 'Isn't it about time we heard this magic voice then!' he hollered.

All the other Boggarts agreed. 'The voice! The voice! Let's hear the voice!'

Nanny looked worried, but the little Thunderboggart was quite happy to show them a few tricks.

First she did a deep hum that made the air buzz like a million angry bees, then a rumble that ran up their legs and made their bellies do cartwheels, followed by a high-pitched squeak that had the same effect on the Boggarts' teeth as chewing silver paper.

'Oooooh! Aaaaah! Ouch! Very nice! Very clever!' said Horris Waggat'wa. 'That's enough of that. What about the earthquake yell?'

The little Thunderboggart shook her head. 'It'd be too dangerous.'

The King was only slightly disappointed, and the other Boggarts were beginning to think it was probably too soon after lunch for that sort of thing.

'Oh well,' said Horris craftily, 'it just remains for me to put you down on my list of special Boggarts with special powers . . . What did you say your name was?'

'None of your business!'

Never had a Temporary King of The Boggarts been so insulted and Boggarts are easily insulted.

'Give some cheek and you'll cry all week!' chanted Seth and Beth.

There was uproar in the palace!

'Take this impudent Thunderboggart to the Temporary Dungeon!' ordered King Waggat'wa.

Nanny pleaded for mercy. Luke kicked the royal shins, but this only made Horris more angry.

'Take this creature away! Lock her up until she apologises and tells us her name!'

Which might have been forever, but the little Thunderboggart was so frightened at the thought of spending the rest of her life in prison that she let fly one of her dangerous earth-shaking yells.

'Yararaarooraraaaaah!'

Every Boggart fell to the floor. The Temporary Palace Walls buckled and shook like jelly, the Temporary Roof started dropping slates, and the Temporary King made a very definite decision to change his last decision.

'Free the Thunderboggart! – But hear this! If she's going to be *like that* with us, we're going to be *like this* with her. Nobody is to speak to her! Everyone is to ignore her! That is the law until I change my mind again!'

The Thunderboggart sat with Nanny and her grandchildren on a stone seat by a fountain that never worked in the Temporary Palace Precinct.

'We'll stay with you,' said Granny. 'The King will

change his temporary mind soon.'

'No!' cried the Thunderboggart. 'You and the rest – you're all the same! You only want to take my magic power away, so get lost!'

'If that's the way you want it!' said Nanny, and walked off with her grandchildren.

Looking back she saw Luke trailing behind as usual, but she didn't shout for him. The little Thunderboggart hunched herself up on the stone seat, put her head between her knees, and curled herself into a ball.

> One day, two days, sunrise and sunset
> She sat on her own and said not a word.
> And no one replied to the nothing she said
> Till the sun rose again on the third.

When she woke up the third day she felt half asleep, hungry, and lonely. But when she opened her eyes properly she realised that she wasn't alone at all – there was a young Boggart sitting on the end of the seat.

'How long have you been here?' she asked. 'You're so quiet.'

'I never left,' said Luke, holding out a brown paper bag. 'D'y'want a crab apple?'

The Thunderboggart took an apple and popped it in her mouth. It tasted delicious . . . sour and mouth-watering. 'Thanks, Luke.'

'That's all right . . . er . . . ?'

'Rachel,' said the Thunderboggart without thinking and then, 'Rachel! Oh no! Yarararooraraaaaah!'

The ground, the trees, the Boggarts' knees . . . everything wobbled at once as once again the world filled up with a hideous, thunderous, eardrum-cracking shout!

Glasses cracked, birds fell off trees, the earth shook, the Temporary Palace finally collapsed, and the crown rolled from Horris Waggat'wa's head.

'Rachel,' she screamed. 'I said my name but my power didn't vanish away.'

Luke hugged Rachel. Rachel hugged Luke.

'Racheeeeeeeeeel!' she shouted with pride and delight. The ground shook again and a tidal wave roared up the river, causing somebody to drop so many stitches that sunbeams danced everywhere on the water.

'Oh. . . . *Rachel*,' sighed Nanny Knitting Needles. 'Is *that* all??'

Tale 4

The BEAUTIFUL BOGGART of TINSELL TOWER

It was a dry windy day in a dry land. It wasn't exactly a desert – a scraggy kind of grass still clung to the hillocks of sand – but it was endless and waterless enough to get lost in forever, and die of thirst.

If you were a bird, say a passing vulture looking down onto that land from the noonday sky, you would have seen two small figures on two legs each, one glinting shiny silver and one matt black. You would have noticed that they were both hopelessly lost, totally unaware of each other, and just about to stagger around the same giant sand dune in opposite directions.

The passing vulture flew on, making a note to call back around suppertime. The black and silver two-legged creatures continued to stumble round the sand dune, their feet trailing, their tongues hanging out (they both had long tongues), and their eyes squinted shut against a wind that seemed to be blasting in all directions at once.

They were bound to bump into each other . . . and they did!

The silver one made a sound that meant, 'Oi! Watch it! Who are you?' but it came out like a strangulated trumpet. The matt black one made a noise that meant much the same thing only it sounded like a dog who's just had his tale stamped on.

The two of them backed off, made more noises at each other for a while, and then the matt black one said, 'I am Padfoot, famous hairy dog-like Boggart feared by all! I am on an Adventurous Quest, and I will slay all who stand in my path!'

'Well, that's an amazing coincidence,' said the

silver one, 'because I am Killmoulis, the famous metallic Boggart with a funnel-mouth! I am on a Mysterious Mission, and I will destroy anyone who stands in my way!'

'And what "mysterious mission" might that be?' demanded Padfoot.

'I'll tell you that when you tell me about your so-called "adventurous quest"!' answered Killmoulis.

The truth was that neither of them had any idea at all what they were doing there, and after a lot of bluster and blather they admitted as much.

'It's the wind,' said Killmoulis, with a sigh like a sad flute. 'It drives all the ideas out of your head. All I really want to do is get out of here!'

'Me too!' grumbled Padfoot. 'If this wind would stop shouting in my ears I'd remember what it was I was looking for.'

Now they had decided not to destroy or slay each other for the time being, the two Boggarts joined forces to try and find some water – and a way out.

As they walked together, heads bent against the wind, they wondered what it might be that had made them come searching in such a wild place.

'Something beautiful, of course . . . something precious . . . it must have been . . .' thought Killmoulis.

'Something wonderful,' said Padfoot aloud. 'Something to make your heart sing!'

'Well there's nothing to make your heart sing around here,' said Killmoulis. And then he looked up, and his heart sang fit to burst.

So intent had the Boggarts been on their wonderings and wanderings that they'd not noticed how the wind had blown itself away, how the scraggy grass had turned to soft meadow . . . and something else, something to make Killmoulis whistle like pan pipes in the spring.

Padfoot sniffed suspiciously, but the fragrant scent in the air made him look, and made his heart leap too.

They were standing in the middle of a meadow, in a garden full of fair flowers. Beside them, a clear stream ran between banks of bluebells. All around were wondrous sights and smells.

Fields of tall sunflowers – daisies and dandelions! Red snapdragons – white snowdrops! Cane fences covered with sweet peas – borders blue with forget-me-nots! Every flower of spring and summer, all growing together!

For a while the two bewildered Boggarts gazed at the garden and forgot their thirst. Then they fell on their knees to drink cool water from the brook.

When they raised their heads again they saw something else to marvel at. At the far end of the meadow was the edge of a wild wood. It looked as deep and dark as most wild woods the Boggarts had known, but there was one very special difference. Out of the middle of the wood, about a mile or so away, rose a tall tower, twinkling magically in the sunlight.

Padfoot gave a bark of recognition: 'It's the legendary Tinsell Tower! Perhaps that was my quest!'

'Look at the top!' cried Killmoulis, and both Boggarts stood amongst the flowers and stared. Far away on the flat roof of the high tower a figure in a white gown was waving urgently.

Killmoulis' funnel mouth opened wide and he

trumpeted a great joy. 'It's the Fabulously Beautiful Boggart Princess of the Tinsell Tower! She's waving at me to come and rescue her!'

Padfoot growled, and spoke proudly. 'This is my Adventurous Quest! It is indeed the Fabulous Princess, who has fallen in love with me, and wishes *me* to rescue her from the Tinsell Tower.'

Killmoulis' silver skin glowed pink with rage. 'It is *my* Mysterious Mission to rescue the Princess and marry her. What's more I'll destroy anyone who stands in my way!'

'And what's more I will slay all who stand in my path!' replied Padfoot, pushing Killmoulis into a privet hedge.

Killmoulis screeched with outrage, and then bounded back, battering Padfoot on the head with his silvery metal arms. Padfoot fell to his knees and tried to bite Killmoulis on the shins.

For half an hour they fought together in the garden. By the end of that time both Boggarts were exhausted, there were flowers uprooted everywhere, and the figure at the top of the tower was waving even more urgently.

'If we carry on like this,' panted Padfoot, 'there'll be neither of us fit to rescue any princesses.'

'Let's just see who gets there first,' said Killmoulis.

So the two Boggarts set off together again. They followed the course of the stream as it flowed into the wood, but came to a sudden stop in front of a barbed wire fence with a sign stapled to it. The sign said, *'Buzz off!'*

'I wonder what that means,' said Killmoulis.

'It means "Go away!", but I'm not going to let any sign stop me from saving the princess.'

'I know what it means, stupid,' snapped Killmoulis, as they climbed painfully over the high fence, 'but what does it *really* mean? When you're on a Mysterious Mission, everything has a Mysterious Meaning!'

So busy was Killmoulis thinking about the mystery of the sign, that he slipped, and had to grab Padfoot to keep his balance.

Padfoot had nothing to hold onto but barbed wire

and thin air, so after a few shrieks and screams two torn and scratched Boggarts rolled off the fence down a slope and landed against the rotten trunk of an old oak.

'Idiot!' groaned Padfoot painfully. 'You and your "Buzz off!" '

'No! Listen!' cried Killmoulis.

From inside the remains of the tree came a loud buzzing noise.

Killmoulis leapt to his feet. 'Buzz off yourself, or come out and fight!'

Padfoot pushed in front of Killmoulis. 'Whoever you are, I challenge you in the name of the Boggart Princess!'

'I challenged first!' yelled Killmoulis.

The mysterious enemy didn't care who was at the front of the queue – it attacked them both together.

'Oo!' 'Arh!' 'Yipe!' 'Yah!'

Yelping with pain, and clapping their hands to different parts of their bodies, the brave Boggarts danced a wild jig as they tried to defend themselves from the swarm of angry hornets that flew from the hollow oak.

It looked as if they'd be stung to death but then Killmoulis dived to the ground, rolled towards the stream and dipped his funnel mouth into the water.

The surface swirled and bubbled as he used his special power to suck in gallons and gallons of liquid. Padfoot was still shouting, still clapping, and still jigging about in circles, when Killmoulis turned . . . and opened fire!

Used in reverse, Killmoulis' funnel mouth became a high-powered water spray that knocked the insects out of the air, and turned the tide of the battle against the hornet hordes.

When it was all over the two Boggarts dropped a tear or two as their stings started to swell, and then raced on through the trees. They might be bruised, they might be scratched and stung – but each of them was determined to reach the princess first.

'Just remember, it was me that saved your life!' panted Killmoulis. 'Just remember to tell that to the princess!'

'I'll tell her who knocked us off the fence!' said Padfoot.

'Alright! Alright! Let's call it quits. Who do you think is holding her prisoner in the tower?'

'A giant I expect, or a dragon, or perhaps she's under one of those magic curses, and the first handsome Boggart to get there and give her a kiss will release her from the evil spell! . . . Yes I expect that's the one. . . . Don't you think so Killmoulis? . . . Killmoulis? . . . Oh no!'

Killmoulis had stopped under a tree. On it was nailed another notice. ' *"Get Lost!"* – What do you think that means?' fluted the funnel-mouthed Boggart.

'Well, *"Buzz off"* meant we got buzzed off, so *"Get lost"* might mean we're about to get lost,' barked his hairy-faced companion. 'But somehow I don't think so.'

'Oh? And why's that, Big Ears?'

'Because we're lost already, Trumpet Lips!'

Padfoot was right. The trees had narrowed around the path and closed in overhead. You couldn't see the tower through the canopy of leaves, and there was no way of knowing which was the right direction.

It felt like being trapped underground. They pushed ahead, taking one leafy passage and then another, twisting and turning around and around till the night fell and the tunnels through the undergrowth turned pitch dark.

'Are you frightened at all?' asked Padfoot.

'Don't be silly. We're Boggarts! We frighten other creatures! Anyway, you don't think the princess is going to marry a yellow-bellied chicken do you?'

There was a whistling in the branches, a screeching in the dark, a breathing behind, and footsteps somewhere ahead rustling through piles of dead leaves.

'I didn't say I was frightened *myself*,' said Padfoot, in a shaky voice. 'I was only worried in case *you* might be!'

'Well, I'm not – am I?' answered a trembling Killmoulis.

It was the worst night either Boggart had ever experienced.

They were tracked by hungry werewolves, driven into dark caves by swarms of blood-sucking vampire bats, haunted by phantoms, ghouls and goblins, bitten by fifty different varieties of poisonous snake, spider and centipede, and then chased until dawn by an army of every kind of frightening and fearsome thing you could envisage.

Luckily for them, all that was in their petrified yellow-belly chicken imaginations, and they emerged alive from the tangle of trees, pale-faced and red-eyed, into a rosy dawn.

They were standing on a road at the far end of the forest. There was another sign on it. It said, *'To the Tinsell Tower,'* pointing one way, and *'To the gardens,'* pointing the other.

'Another sign!' said Killmoulis.

'You and your signs!' growled Padfoot. 'I'll tell you what that sign means! It means we could have come here by the main road, Metal Brain!'

Then they remembered the princess and ran towards the tower, each desperate to arrive there first.

Killmoulis was in the lead, but he ground to a sudden halt before the Tower Gate. Nailed to it was another sign.

Keep out! Beware of the cat!

'That's silly!' thought the tin-snouted one. 'It's usually a dog!'

Next minute he was running back the other way, towards Padfoot. Padfoot wondered why his rival had changed his mind about the princess, until he noticed a large cat bounding down the road after him . . . the kind of large cat that's usually called a Jaguar.

It looked like curtains this time for the deadly double duo, but the Hairy-skinned Boggart hadn't used his special power yet. Howling aloud from the

OF THE
CAT!

depth of his belly, he turned himself into a Giant Black Dog, with very spikey teeth.

The Jaguar screeched to a stop. Its fur stood on end like any old alley cat, and then it ran straight up to the top of the nearest tree!

'Now I've saved *your* life,' said Padfoot, changing back from dog to dog-like. But Killmoulis hadn't waited to thank him. He was racing for the tower and the princess.

Padfoot chased after his rival, all weariness forgotten. Killmoulis had already begun to climb the trailing tinsell, but Padfoot struggled after him – hot on his heels – so that both Boggarts hauled themselves over the parapet at exactly the same moment.

There was the Fabulously Beautiful Boggart Princess, and no dragons or giants in sight. Each of the Boggarts declared his undying love, asked for her hand in marriage, and offered a big sloppy kiss to release her from the evil spell.

'It was me you were waving to, wasn't it?' whined Padfoot.

'No! It was me!' wailed Killmoulis.

The princess spoke. 'It was *both* of you!'

'*Both* of us?' said the astonished Boggarts.

'Yes! *Both* of you!' repeated the princess. 'I was waving at you to get off my flowerbeds! . . . And while you're at it, *Buzz Off* out of my woods! *Keep Out* of my Private Tower, and *Get lost* before I have you arrested for attacking my pussycat!'

Then the Fabulous Princess kicked the dumbstruck Boggarts through the inner door, calling after them as they bounced down the stairs:

'Can't you two boneheads read signs?!!!'

Tale 5

MAD JEN IRONSIDES of BOGGARTS END

In summer it was slightly warm. In winter it was a bit chilly. In autumn and spring there was light drizzle, but never enough for an umbrella. The weather in the Wyrmslow valley was always more or less average, and that's how the people of Wyrmslow preferred it.

Through the Wyrmslow valley ran the River Wyrm. It wound its comfortable way once around Wyrmslow Village Church, and then truckled off towards the sea, as well behaved and unadventurous as the villagers themselves.

Which is why Jen Ironsides Johnson was having a blazing row with her parents.

'I'm bored and I've had enough!' shouted Jen. 'Do you understand what I'm saying?'

'Yes, yes! But why do you have to leave home?' asked Mr Johnson for the tenth time.

'I've told you why! Because nothing ever happens here, and nothing ever will!'

Her dad pondered and twizzled his beard. 'There's that vampire lives in Wyrmslow churchyard . . .'

'You know very well he's a vegetarian!' said Jen.

Jen's mum had an inspiration. 'Once there was a waterspout that swept down the river, with a Monstrous Ogre spinning around on the top! *That* wasn't boring!'

'That was *years* ago!' sighed Jen.

'Well, what about the Council Gardens?' asked her dad suddenly.

'What about them?'

'They're quite nice,' said her dad in a feeble voice and gave up the argument.

Her mum didn't surrender so easily. 'Suppose we

do what you say! Suppose we give you all your inheritance – all the bags of gold your father and I have stuffed up the chimney for you all these years. What are you going to do with it, eh? Just where exactly do you plan going, my girl?'

Jen laughed. 'I'm off to the hills!'

'And what do you mean by that?' demanded her father, as he realised with a terrible shock that his daughter was seriously planning to leave Wyrmslow.

'I mean I'm going to live on Hobbs Hill!' said Jenny. 'There's an old broken-down hut about half-way up on a rocky ledge. I'm going to make a house of it!'

'That's ridiculous!' said her mother.

'That's ridiculous!' repeated her father. 'There's only Boggarts and goats up there. How will you live?'

'Perhaps I'll keep goats,' suggested Jen.

'Never mind the goats!' said Jen's mother. 'What about the Boggarts?!'

'Boggarty Boggarty Boo! I want to be friends with you!' sang Jen.

Her parents were horrified.

And so were all the villagers of Wyrmslow when they heard about Jen's plan. Some of them called round to pay her a friendly visit.

'It is well known,' declared the Lord Mayor of Wyrmslow, 'that there is all kinds of weather up on Hobbs Hill. Anyone who lived up there would die of *Chilblains* or *Heat Lumps*!'

'Hooey Fooey!' said Jen.

'It is also well known,' declared the Wyrmslow Senior Librarian, consulting a heavy old book with terrifying black-and-white drawings, 'that Hobbs Hill is over-run with Boggarts,

Wild and Witchery,
Tricksy, Twitchery,
Hairy, Tattery,
Mad as a Hattery!

And anyone who saw such Boggarts, in the real life so to speak, would probably die of *A Nervous Rash.*'

'Flimflam Flapdoodle!' said Jen.

'Furthermore, it is also well known that several of these Boggarts are well known to us!' declared Wyrmslow's Chief Constable. 'Scantly Mab, Hobthross the Thresher, Hob Headless, Gabriel Ratchet, Peg O'Lantern, Dicky Doodle, Lazy Lob . . . and that's to name but a few!'

'And they're led,' said Wyrmslow's Chief Magistrate, 'by Bloodnose Redcap, the most Fearsome Cut-Throat Hill-Bandit Boggart of them all! Anyone who mixed with the likes of him would probably die of *Germs* or *An Accident With A Sharp Knife!*'

Jen looked a little worried and the Assistant Deputy Headmistress of Wyrmslow School for the Daughters of Gentlefolk seized her opportunity.

'What is even more well known, and even more to the point, is that your legs don't work for walking – Jen Ironsides Johnson! Hobbs Hill is *extremely* steep, and it will be *impossible* for you to get up and down the slope in your *wheelchair*!'

Everyone was very relieved to hear this and went home.

Jen went to bed and thought about what they'd said for a long while. She came, at last, to her *own* conclusion:

'Hocus Pocus! Prittle prattle
Mumbo Jumbo! Tittle tattle
Phoney baloney, Flannel and Hype!
Hogwash Tommyrot, Bosh Tosh Tripe!'

Then she got out of bed again, took her gold from up the chimney, and went off in her wheelchair to do some organising.

First she bought a big fat sketching pad and a pencil, and then sat for a while in the Council Gardens, drawing a plan and making a list.

Then she went to Arkwrights Engineering Emporium and ordered half a mile of strong chain, some huge gear wheels, a giant motor engine, concrete and iron posts, and lots of other such stuff that had to come in huge lorries from far away.

The villagers watched the big trucks come and go, and watched the equipment pile up at the bottom of Hobbs Hill.

The Mayor, and the Chief Constable, and the Senior Librarian, and the Magistrate, and especially the Assistant Deputy Headmistress all decided that Jen had flipped her lid.

' "Mad Jen Ironsides!" That's what they call you!' said her father, but Jen didn't give a dry fig from last Christmas what they called her.

Next she hired some surveyors and mechanical engineers and builders and bricklayers, and had them use the stuff she'd bought, to construct the thing she'd drawn.

While they were doing that she had a path constructed that wound round and round and down the hill.

When all the work was finished, Jen used the last of her money to buy a herd of goats and put an advert in the *Wyrmslow Weekly Express*.

> *Mad Jen Ironsides invites everyone to the opening of the most impossibly exciting thing to happen anywhere near Wyrmslow for years and years and* ***years!***

They didn't want to come, but they couldn't keep away.

The Mayor, and the Chief Constable, and the Senior Librarian, and the Magistrate, and especially the Assistant Deputy Headmistress all watched and wondered as Jen hitched her wheelchair to the chain at the bottom of Hobbs Hill, and pressed the button for the motor to start.

The engine fired. The gear wheels turned. The chain went up the hill, and so did Jen Ironsides Johnson.

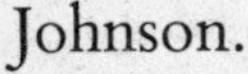

'That's all very well, and all very clever-clever,' said the Assistant Deputy. 'But how does the poor foolish girl expect to get safely down again?'

'I expect she'll put the motor in reverse,' said the Mayor wisely, but he was wrong. Next minute they were both diving into a ditch, as Jen wooshed past them in her wheelchair, coming off the end of her spiral path at about forty miles an hour.

The Chief Constable charged her with speeding in a built-up area, but the case was so complicated that the Magistrate had to go on a long holiday.

After that, Jen moved into her new house, and started looking after the goats. Her mother and father came to see her, gave her some net curtains for a house-warming present, and ordered a crate of goats milk even though they didn't like the taste of it.

'We like to see you happy,' said her mum.

'You're not so crazy,' said her dad.

But most of the villagers were slow to change their minds. 'You watch out!' they cried as they scattered out of the path of her flying wheelchair. 'You watch out or the Boggarts'll get you, Mad Jen Ironsides!'

Jen wondered why she hadn't seen a single Boggart since she'd moved in, but the Wyrmslow Senior Librarian pulled out another dusty old book, and explained everything:

From Midwinter Day to Midsummer's Eve,
The Hobbs Hill Boggarts take their leave.
So if you'd like to die of a fright,
Bide your time till Midsummer's Night!

'That's this very night!' said Jen.

'Awful coincidence!' said the Librarian. 'Perhaps you should go back home to live with your parents.'

But when dusk fell Jen was up on a rocky ledge with the goats, watching the dark clouds gather over Hobbs Hill.

'I think there's going to be weather,' she said. Then the rain fell, the lightning flashed, the thunder rolled, and Jen Ironsides wheeled out into the storm, shouting aloud with excitement.

'I like thunder!
I like rain!
Gurgle urgle
Down the drain!'

The thunder rocked and rolled for her. The rain came down by bathfulls, and then another cry answered hers, a high pitched scream calling clear through the storm from further down the hill.

'Take to your heels! Run and hide!
Many from fear of me have died!
The longest day is over and done!
I'm Bloodnose Redcap! Here I come!'

Redcap! Jen had heard the name before, and felt a chill of fear as the words of the Magistrate came to her mind. '*Germs!* or *An Accident With A Sharp Knife!*'

Then she remembered who she was, and all that she'd done and dared to do, and she shouted back into the darkness:

'Bloodnose Redcap – I'm here to stay!
I'm Mad Jen Ironsides! Out of my way!'

With a yell, she launched herself down the hill as

fast as she could – helping the wheels to turn by spinning them with her hands – round and round and faster and faster – until she saw him there on the path ahead – the grey cloak – the red cap – but she didn't stop.

'Look out!' she cried, when it was almost too late, and Bloodnose Redcap, the fiercest Boggart of the High Hills, went head over heels rolling down the slope.

Jen carried on speeding towards Wyrmslow Village. Redcap picked himself up and ran after her. He was easily insulted, but not for hundreds of years had he felt quite so mortified.

'An insult to one is an insult to all!' he cried, and all the other Midsummer Boggarts heard his call and scampered down Hobbs Hill after him.

Doors were slammed in Wyrmslow. Windows were bolted.

Bloodnose Redcap was prancing down the High Street in a rage! 'Jen Ironsides! Where is she? Where is Mad Jen? Tell me where she is or I'll set your houses ablaze!'

Redcap wasn't Ball-O-Fire, the Flame Boggart. He didn't even have a box of matches on him, but the cowardly villagers of Wyrmslow weren't to know that.

'She's down by the Council Gardens,' whimpered the Lord Mayor.

Redcap jumped over the park railings, climbed like a cat up a tree, crawled along a branch, and then launched himself through the air directly onto Jen Ironsides who was wheeling underneath.

The chair overturned and the two of them fell out, gripping each other hand and arm, rolling and wrestling in the grass.

The rest of the Boggarts were arriving now, and they formed a noisy circle round Jen and Redcap.

Hob Headless was there, Cappelthwaite with his Crook, Gabriel Ratchet that rides the Helm Wind, Dicky Doodle, Lazy Lob, and Peg O'Lantern illuminating the whole scene with her weird flickering lights.

'An insult to one is an insult to all!' they chanted.

Redcap had the crowd behind him. He seized Jen's left arm and shoved it behind her back. Jen screamed with pain, but managed to grab Redcap's ear with her right hand and twist hard. Then it was Redcap's turn to cry. The other Boggarts were getting more and more excited. They'd never seen anyone, Boggart or human, try to wrestle with Redcap and they wanted to see the outcome.

They didn't have long to wait.

Redcap mostly relied on hot air and bad publicity, but he had a fearsome grip. He caught hold of Jen's right hand, and forced her fingers free of his ear-lobe. Next moment he had both of Jen's arms up behind her back!

'It's all over!' cried Scantly Mab, and the Boggarts surged forward –

– and stopped in amazement. Jen had very little wrestling experience, but pushing her wheelchair had given her stronger than average muscle power.

Incredibly – inch by inch – she was pulling her arms down her back. With a final wrench she turned about and applied a Full Nelson to Redcap's neck.

Bloodnose was done for – face down in the damp grass, crying for help. Jen had won, but she wasn't safe. If the Boggarts attacked her all together, there was nothing she could do.

But the Boggarts didn't attack. They laughed.

'I've always wanted to see Redcap meet his match,' said Cappelthwaite. 'Now he's been bested perhaps he'll stop shouting and boasting round the hills every summer.'

Even Redcap had to laugh now, or look foolish. The Boggarts lifted Jen up and carried her in a victory procession along Wyrmslow High Street and up Hobbs Hill. The Helm Wind blew. Peg O'Lantern's Dobbie-Lights flickered through the streets, and Hob Headless sang his head off:

'Boggarty Boggarty Boo!
We want to be friends with you!
Wild and Witchery,
Tricksy, Twitchery,
Hairy, Tattery,
Mad as a Hattery,
Boggarty Boggarty Boo!'

The Wyrmslow villagers kept themselves locked up safe and tight for two weeks. When they finally put their noses out of their doors, they could hear the sound of a wild party coming from half way up Hobbs Hill – a sound they still hear most Midsummer Saturday nights, from a house which Jen has named, more in affection than in triumph, 'Boggarts End!'

A Boggart Spotter's Guide

featuring

NOTES ON BOGGARTS,

THEIR INDIVIDUAL

PECULIARITIES,

and the

PRONUNCIATION OF

THEIR NAMES.

BOGGARTS MENTIONED IN 'BOGGART SANDWICH'

JACK IRONTEETH
A mining Boggart. Jack lives in a deserted mine on Hobsmoor Common. His metal teeth contain fluorspar which makes them shine in the dark. His teeth sometimes get a bit rusty, but they'd be less chipped and cracked if he gave up chewing coal.

KILLMOULIS
Pronounced Killmoolee.

A silvery metallic skinned Boggart, with a funnel-mouth. Has a voice that can trumpet and flute and wail like a range of brass instruments. His funnel mouth can suck and blow at high speed, rather like a sophisticated modern vacuum cleaner. Sometimes acts as Temporary Herald to Horris Waggat'wa, Temporary King of The Boggarts.

Killmoulis has a sister of the same name who lives in The Wild Forest in the Land at the Edge of the World. They haven't met since they were separated at birth.

TATTERY BOGGARTS
As the name suggests, they are wild, ragged and hairy. They usually live in trees and bushes, and are probably the most changeable in their ways, and the most easily offended of all Boggarts. Tattery Boggarts like space and freedom. Like many other

Boggarts they are sometimes able to make themselves invisible. Female Tattery Boggarts are the most fearsome.

SCANTLY MAB

A powerful Boggart from the High Hills. The Weaver of Fate. She is the daughter of Habetrot, the Spinner of Fate.

HOBTHROSS

Pronounced **Hob**thross.

The Boggart Thresher. She can take many shapes, somctimes male, sometimes female. Whatever she looks like she usually wears yellow and green, and a bunch of straw as a decoration.

In the old days she was supposed to stuff chaff into the mouths of children who wouldn't eat their greens, and is still renowned today for her hatred of fussiness, snobbery, and pomposity.

PADFOOT

A dog-like Boggart. Hairy, and matt black in colour. Padfoot has the power to change himself into a large dog with pointed teeth when necessary. He sometimes follows travellers to warn of impending danger or death.

NANNY KNITTING NEEDLES

A Waterboggart, with webbed hands and feet. Once she had a fearsome reputation, but now she lives more or less peacefully by the River Wyrm with her four Waterboggart grandchildren, Beth, Seth, Ruth, and Luke. Waterboggarts have the special power to knit the river into swirls, whirlpools, even waves and waterspouts. They are very gregarious and like to dine out together on pondslime, watersnail pie, and suchlike savouries.

JINNY GREENTEETH

A Swamp Boggart, who lives in a hut on stilts in the middle of Niffy Marshes. Suffers from bad teeth, and a morbid fear of dentists. Very striking in appearance – puce-green face, snot-green eyes, slime-green hair and moss-green teeth. She has a reputation for catching travellers – especially dentists – and pulling them into the mire.

BLOODNOSE REDCAP

'The most terrible Hill-Bandit Boggart of them all.' The fearsome leader of a gang known as The Midsummer Boggarts. Never baths. Wears a grey cloak and a red cap. He is fond of giving himself bad publicity. He once put around a story that his cap was dyed red with blood he had spilt, and now it's in all the library books. Used to carry a sharp knife, but found he kept cutting himself with it. Very powerful wrestler, but not quite as good as he says he is.

HORRIS WAGGAT'WA

Rhymes with Maggot star, and samovar.

Horris Waggat'wa, The Temporary King of The Boggarts, has floppy ears and a terrible curiosity. Actually he is a very ordinary home-loving Boggart. He was chosen to be Temporary King because no one else fancied the job. Always changing his mind.

CAPPELTHWAITE
A shepherd Boggart with a magical crook. Good at finding or losing beasts, people, and things.

HOB HEADLESS
Very smartly dressed, which is considered out of order for a Boggart, but Hob is tolerated because he hasn't got a head to go with the rest of his body. He has, however, got the finest voice of all Boggarts – another mystery! He has the power to make light things heavy, and if you sit on a stone he can make you so heavy you can't get up again.

BALL-O-FIRE, THE FLAME BOGGART
Ball-O-Fire has long red hair that sticks out in all directions, and thin and bony legs and arms. She has the special power to turn into ball lightning and fly or hover in the air.

THUNDERBOGGARTS
Thunderboggarts have the power to make all kinds of loud and interesting noises, but especially to be able to do an earthquake-shout that causes the ground to shake. Some Thunderboggarts believe that they may lose their powers if they tell their name.

HOB-LIE-BY-THE-FIRE
A very domestic Boggart who likes to lie invisibly by other people's fires. He's very clumsy, and responsible for spilling cups of coffee, and many other minor unexplained household accidents.

LAZY LOB
A younger more outgoing version of Hob-Lie-By-The-Fire. Causes disruption at the workplace and especially out of doors. Once had a competition with Hob-Lie-By-The-Fire to see who was the most indolent.

GABRIEL RATCHET
A Hunting Boggart that rides the Helm Wind. Has the power to follow faint scents and smells.

THE FABULOUSLY BEAUTIFUL BOGGART PRINCESS OF TINSELL TOWER
A legendary Boggart who is supposed to be trapped in the tower until rescued by a handsome Boggart Prince, who will climb up the trailing tinsell and save her from the whatever.

PEG O'LANTERN
Her magical Dobbie-Lights are sometimes seen at night, dancing in the dark. She's seldom seen herself, but sometimes manifests as a gentle elderly lady with a headscarf.

DICKY DOODLE (OF DOODLESHIRE)
A silly tricksy Boggart, who delights in playing daft practical jokes. Often mistaken for a ghost. He is believed to be the origin of all the bad jokes that can't be traced to their source.

BOGGARTS NOT MENTIONED IN 'BOGGART SANDWICH' BUT WHOM YOU MAY HAVE SEEN

HABETROT
Pronounced Habbytrot.

The Spinner of Fate, she lives in the hills with Scantly Mab, her daughter.

TRASH
A long-bearded old boggart who hangs around alleyways and back gardens. Wraps his beard round and round him to keep warm. Also wears old clothes and old rubbish for warmth and decoration.

DUNNEY
A thieving Boggart with shiny hair, beady eyes and long arms. Very fond of horses, bicycles, cars and all means of transport. When he rides them they vanish. Has lots of relations called Little Dunnies who live in attics and cellars and down the back of sofas. They collect pens and odd socks and other small articles.

HEDLEY KOW
A very frightening Boggart Cow, now very vain since her mention in folklore, guide books etc.

THE BARGHEIST
Nobody knows much about the Bargheist. Nobody dares speak to it.

Don't you!

ADDENDUM

The Bogeyman

Many Boggarts don't believe in fairies, so it's not surprising that they're doubtful about Bogeymen.

Some will tell you a tale about a tribe of Waterboggarts who went underground millions of years ago, and still 'pop up' to cause mischief.

Other Boggarts insist that Bogeymen are just made-up monsters to frighten children. But in a dusty old book in Wyrmslow Central Library it says:

The Bogeyman has the Mind of a Man,
The Hands and Feet and Stride of a Man.
There's nought more Fair or Frightful than
The Bogeyman!